COUNCIL & CO.
WELCOME TO
P.OLE
GIGI SHOE

Council & CO Present:

Welcome to Pole

by: Gigi Shoe

Welcome to Pole

Gigi Shoe

For rights and permissions, please contact:
Gigi Shoe
gigishoe.com

ISBN: 9781968852054

For all the December Birthdays

Sunday

Stepping outside smelled like snow. The cold winter breeze swept through Main Square as Marty Saint Claus inhaled a deep breath; pine trees and cinnamon filling her senses. A snowflake landed against her eyelids; face pointed upward to feel the last warmth of the sun as it disappeared behind gray clouds.

Children's laughter and the singing of carolers drew her attention to the skating rink. Decorative iron fencing surrounded the skaters with a giant Christmas tree planted in the center. Adventurers crossed the bridge to reach Mayor Kringle, who led a countdown. Reaching ONE, he flipped a switch lighting thousands of bulbs around the tree.

The crowd *oohed* and *ahhed* on cue.

Strands of twinkling lights ran from the top of the Christmas tree to the surrounding iron lampposts, lighting the rink. More were zigzagging back and forth between the two rows of brick tourist shops that made up the town of Pole. The square was lined with cobblestone walkways, benches draped in large red bows, doors laden with decorative wreaths, and windows full of colorful displays enticing Adventurers to spend, Spend, SPEND!

To Marty's left was *Santa's Workshop*. A line of children perused the windows, cheeks pressed against the glass, watching the elves inside build toys while waiting patiently for their turn upon Santa's lap. Beyond *Santa's Workshop*, at the end of the square, stood *Mr. & Mrs. Claus' Mansion Tours*; a large two-story, brick monstrosity that Marty curled her upper lip at.

Capping the opposite end of the square, the belltower atop the *Visitors Center* gave five low tones—*gong, gong, gong, gong, gong*—signaling the evening hour.

One week left until Christmas.

The best week of the year!

Well, not according to Marty.

She hated the week before Christmas because the holiday never *ended* when you worked in Pole where every week was the week before Christmas. Every Sunday began on December 20th and every Saturday ended December 26th—the day after Christmas being the only acceptable day to not change your pajamas, eat leftover food, and lounge unproductively.

And the tourists were worse. Always walking around in a constant state of dreamlike beauty commenting about how *lucky* they'd be to live there or how *wonderful* it must be to always celebrate Christmas!

It was disgustingly irritating to Marty.

"New guy incoming," chirped the voice of Chestnut on her right. Marty was twice the age of the teen elf and knew Chestnut only pretended be just as miserable even though the elf secretly loved Christmas.

Out of curiosity, Marty turned, spotting the new Santa who greeted Mayor Kringle at the Workshop, shaking his hand exuberantly. The newcomer wasn't in costume yet with his predecessor sitting on the throne, smiling, and *ho-ho-ho*ing for the children, but he was young—hardly a hair on his chin—was that a pimple?—barely out of whelping school.

"The first time a kid wets themselves on his lap, he'll be out of here." Marty muttered, shaking her head at the scene. It was quite sad. They went through a lot of Santa's. The Adventurers were brutal, demanding year-round cheer at all hours of the day and night.

"I'll get Nan to start a betting pool," Chezi replied with a nod. Nan was *not* going to start a betting pool. The old woman was too nice for that and truly, genuinely, *liked* Christmas. Nan was more likely to bake welcoming cookies and give an encouraging pep talk.

"Not worth it," Marty mumbled and walked in the direction of the *Bakery*, diagonal from the Ornament store she occupied and directly across from the Workshop. It was her turn to pick up lunch from the café elves.

While Marty hated Christmas, she absolutely detested the *Bakery* because she detested Cleo. The elf was *bubbly*—no matter how ungodsly the hour. Not only that but Cleo always looked meticulous. Her golden curls fell in perfect ringlets around slightly pointed ears and an angelic round face. Her full lips were naturally pink and large, almond eyes, were bright and welcoming to the Adventurers.

Pushing thirty, Marty felt like an old maid in comparison. Her hair straight and dark, though leaning grayer and whiter with each passing week. Freckles covered her pale skin, thin, frowning lips and dark, narrow eyes. A pointed, awkward chin and nose both caused Adventurers to ask if she was constipated or upset. She wasn't either of those because she wasn't an elf with glittery skin, compliant disposition, and habitual cheeriness.

Marty was so lost in thought, gathering quick retorts to imaginary scenarios that she walked right across the Workshop lawn, catching the attention of Mayor Kringle.

"Mistletoe! Mistletoe Saint Claus!" Mayor Kringle's hands waved wildly her direction. With his red trimmed suit and overly large black top-hat, he could stir up quite a scene.

Pausing in her tracks and pasting a smile on her face, she took a steadying breath before turning to face the men.

"Mayor Kringle!" she greeted because she was *technically* still in her ballerina costume—pink tutu and tights, and there were *technically* Adventurers watching—she couldn't spoil the magic. She may hate Christmas for personal reasons, but she wasn't cold-hearted enough to ruin it for the kids—yet.

"I'm so glad I ran into you," the mayor sang galivanting over to her, his legs gliding at an angle as if dancing. "I want to introduce our newest, err—*cousin*—," everyone was a *cousin* in front of the Adventurers, "—to you and see if you'd get him settled into his residency."

"I would but I'm only on a quick lunch break," Marty shrugged her shoulders, signaling an *aw, shucks,* smile.

"Perfect! You may introduce him to Miss Evergreen; she'll happily escort him around town!" Mayor Kringle clapped his hands excitedly and danced away. The mayor never caught onto her sarcasm and thought her *simply a delight!*

"—and her bed." Marty slipped under her breath before turning back to the newcomer who *did* hear. His stunning ice-blue eyes met hers, widening in surprise as a smile spread across his face. She noticed he was barely taller than her own height as she scanned him up and down: scrawny build that will fill out in another ten years, boyish youth that was annoyingly cute but irritating, and as she suspected—not a whisker in sight along his pimple-lined jawline.

"Nolan," his voice squeaked holding out a hand to shake.

"No-land?" Marty inquired purposefully mispronouncing, "You'll fit right in with that tag."

"*No-lan,* actually—and thank you, I plan to fit in quite well. You are?" his eyes sparkled teasingly with a cheeky grin and his fingers wiggled, waiting.

"Charmed," ignoring the hand since she'd probably crush it in her palm.

"Is that your name? Because I just met someone named Miracle a few minutes ago so now I feel like I need to double check." Nolan lifted a thumb over his shoulder, pointing backwards.

She changed her mind, he'd last two days.

"House is that way," she nodded toward the Mansion looming behind the Workshop where candy-cane fence lined the snow-covered yard.

"Is that all for me?" Nolan nervously chuckled at the size of the windows and gabled roof.

"Listen, if you're going to play the part, you might consider eating—a lot." Marty looked at his gaunt stomach, unsure if the Santa costume had enough padding so he'd appear *huggable*.

"If you'll show me where lunch is, I'll be happy to eat." He raised his eyebrows. Their bushy size didn't add to the charm.

"Okay, we're done here." Marty turned on her heel.

"That was a bad joke—err, comment," Nolan stuttered under his breath.

"There are three places to eat in town, the *Bakery*, *Hotel Restaurant*, or *Moms Coffee & Kitchen*.

The town is only one street from Mansion to Museum. You can figure the rest out yourself." She left him to do just that not expecting him to follow, kicking up snow as he stumbled behind.

"I'm sorry, I didn't mean for that to be awkward—this is my first job, and I don't really know—" he rambled. If there was one thing Marty hated more than Christmas, it was needless chatter. She didn't care about your cat, she didn't want to hear your babies babbling, and *no*—she wasn't interested in the flower your cactus finally bloomed. Those conversations were soul-suckingly pointless and painful. "—but then I took a wrong turn when I was driving to the portal and got stuck in a snow pile but thankfully it was just over the next ridge—" he continued as she paused to open the Bakery door.

Nolan stepped up behind her, his body filling the space—filling *too* much of the space—and she turned abruptly, finding herself staring at his throat.

He had to catch himself against the doorframe to prevent bumping into her. She looked him over again then met his eyes. The same startling blue but he looked...taller.

"What? Is there something on my face?" Nolan asked in surprise.

She narrowed her eyebrows. Her head was messing with her. Or maybe it was the way he leaned over—*over*—her body. Something was different. *He* was different.

"Are you okay? Do you need help?" his voice was deeper than a moment before. Marty's stomach jumped at the sound, vastly different from the irritating squeak. His hand reached out and squeezed her upper arm gently, concern on his face.

"Don't touch me," she snapped and rolled her arm out of his hold. It was annoyingly comforting. This guy didn't know anything about her—and he *wasn't* taller.

"I'm sorry, you're right. That was rude of me." Nolan held his hands up, stepping backwards as the door behind Marty was pulled open from inside.

"Mistletoe Saint Claus, *Who* is your friend?" the voice of Cleo sang from behind Marty.

"Mistletoe? Is that your name?" Nolan smiled at Marty without acknowledging the elf.

"Marty," she muttered, a slight snarl at Cleo pulled Marty into the Bakery by the sleeve of her tulle jacket—the only piece allowed to accompany the short, stiff, silk tutu. Perhaps it wasn't the best idea to remain in costume when she fetched lunch.

"You *must* introduce me!" Cleo faced Nolan who followed them inside, her hands on her waist, hips swinging. As expected, Cleo looked immaculate in an adorable bell sleeved white and red striped dress. Matching apron tied around her waist; hoopskirt puffing out, hiding her feet beneath. Her hair was in two curls upon her head, with a baker hat sitting between them. She looked adorable and *comfortable*; Marty fought envy as she pulled against her corset bodice.

The boy—guy, man—smiled warmly toward Cleo and held his hand out to shake. She placed her palm delicately in his and fluttered her eyelids. Marty snorted at her response.

"Nolan Tyme, new Sant—"

"Shhh!" both Marty and Cleo hissed before he could continue. Everyone within earshot would be fired by the Council & CO. if *that* name was casually said out loud. It was important to stay in character around Adventurers and Nolan wasn't in costume.

"I need lunch," Marty turned away, leaving Nolan to the vices of Cleo. She marched straight for the lunch fridge where pre-packaged cold sandwiches waited. Pulling several out for Chezi and Nan back at the Ornament Shop, she also grabbed dessert and drinks, balancing everything within her arms.

She turned to see Nolan and Cleo laughing, the elves hand grazing his forearm flirtatiously as she leaned forward, shoulders hunching inward so her sweetheart neckline showed more cleavage. Nolan's shoulders looked broader. Marty shook her head; *positive* he had been bony moments ago. His face also appeared to have a five o'clock shadow where before it had been as clean as a reindeer's nostril.

"Stop doing that!" Marty stalked across the Bakery and pointed a finger at Nolan's face— his *stupidly* pretty face, dropping a sandwich in the process.

"Doing what?" his eyes widened like her finger might curse him.

"Mistletoe you are a menace!" Cleo hissed through her teeth, still holding a smile though her eyes screamed anger and annoyance while Marty bent to retrieve the fallen food.

When she straightened, she was left with no choice but to pass between Nolan and Cleo to exit. Nolan who wasn't going to admit to playing eye tricks with his appearance.

"Wait, wait—" Nolan reached out at the last moment and blocked her path. "—I was just meeting your friend—"

"Oh, Mistletoe and I aren't friends," Cleo smirked and sandwiched herself in between Marty and Nolan, forcing her back into the Bakery while juggling the items in her arms. "—she's the village stray, after all."

Marty stiffened. Cleo had been calling her a *stray* since they were children.

"Stray?" Nolan repeated, glancing between the two women.

"Well of course," Cleo giggled. "She's an orphan—dropped on the doorstep of the Claus' house thirty-some years ago with a note—" but Marty pushed past Nolan, hard enough to knock him off-balance, abruptly leaving to skip the end of the story.

Monday

"I have a theory," Nolan announced walking up to the counter of the *Little Snowglobe Ornament Shop*. He *rap-tap-tapped* his hands along the top, forcing Marty to take a step back without glancing up from the book she read in her hands. Today she wore tweed knickerbockers with a white button-downed shirt, frilled collar and cuffs, and a maroon cummerbund complete with white knee-high socks and black leather shoes. She wore her hair in a sideways bun, a tweed cap on her head, and leaned against a golf club.

"Did you finally escape the clutches of Miss Evergreen?" she muttered ignoring the customer that stood in line behind Nolan with a basketful of purchases. Marty never really helped at the store but puttered around glaring and sighing deeply.

"Hello! Did you find everything okay?" Chestnut's gentle voice perked up to welcome the customer, gesturing for them to approach the counter as Nolan stepped aside.

"I did, she was quite informative about the village and showed me around the entire square during the opening ceremony last night." Nolan followed, parallel to the counter, as Marty walked away. The large wooden counter wrapped around the entirety of the store forming a U-shape that faced the double doors into the street. Marty aimed to get as far away from Nolan as possible with no end point in mind.

"I don't technically start my duties until tomorrow. The ice-skating rink looked like a lot of fun so I was thinking when you get off, you might be interested—" Nolan was still dodging other customers, swimming upstream amongst the crowd in the shop, as he kept pace.

"No." Marty didn't look up from her reading, but he distracted her enough that she lost her place several times.

"Wait, yesterday, let me explain—" Nolan tried to explain.

"I'm not interested." Marty snapped her book shut. She turned abruptly, trying to catch him off guard but met his eyes—still piercing blue—and found herself frozen.

Nolan changed again—the beard was longer than yesterday, his hair fuller and lighter—gross. Did his shoulders seem extra wide? Almost too wide? His legs looked more profound, not gangly as they had before.

"Have I offended you in some way?" Nolan asked, a hand against his chest in protest. He leaned over the counter but didn't touch her forearm.

"Yes," she nodded without smiling and tucked the book against her own chest, gripping the golf club tighter.

"Such as...?" he urged, circling his wrist and hand while waiting. Her green eyes stared pointedly at him for several long, drawn out, seconds before he caught on. "You won't be telling me...because you're being sarcastic?"

"Be nice." Chestnut tsked walking up beside Marty. "I'm Chestnut, or Chezi, good to meet you."

"Likewise," Nolan shook her hand with a nod. "I'm the new San—"

"Shhh—" Chestnut reminded him; a single finger against her lips before he could finish his sentence. A little girl and her grandmother moved behind a shelf of ornaments, out of earshot.

"Gods, sorry—I keep forgetting!" Nolan blushed and waved his hand close to his temple. Marty certainly agreed he was crazy.

"You should go skating, Marty." Chestnut urged reminding all of them about Nolan's offer hanging in the air.

"The *Main Square Tree Decorating Ceremony* is today," Marty reminded Chestnut, as if every villager didn't have the weekly schedule memorized. Sunday was the tree lighting festival which kicked off the first full day of the *Week Before Christmas*. Monday gave the Adventurers the opportunity to decorate the Christmas tree with personalized ornaments or ornaments bought in the village—hence the rush of shoppers that day.

"What is the ceremony called?" Nolan questioned watching her face intently.

"The *Main Square Tree Decorating Ceremony*." Marty muttered dryly. She stared at Nolan and wondered if he really was that incompetent.

"It's usually crowded," Chestnut explained. "Marty's not a big fan of—"

"Tight places?" Nolan suggested. He looked like an alternate offer was on his tongue.

"People." Marty interrupted annoyed by Nolan's continued presence and his blue eyes that twinkled as if they shared an inside joke. She wondered how hard she needed to swing the golf club at his skull to cause maximum damage.

"Is that a *no* on ice skating?" Nolan clarified. Marty's eyebrows rose and Chestnut let out an adorably awkward elfish laugh before dragging her friend away.

Tuesday

Nolan's hair was darker and long enough that it flopped sideways over his eyes. He shook the snowflakes off with a weathered hand, flipping his bangs back as he walked inside the shop. His stomach had grown and now flopped past his belt buckle. A gray sweater covered the paunch and gave a cuddly illusion. The blue of his scarf made his eyes twinkle with glee. He flashed a bright, merry smile underneath a full beard that melted the knees of every woman in his vicinity.

Except for Marty.

Marty rolled her eyes, her face the only thing visible behind the oval shape cut into the center of a golden, five-pointed star costume, arms pinned to her side limiting her movements. As such, when Marty rotated away from the entryway scene Nolan caused with his white teeth, she failed to see the toy displays on either side of her body.

Her costume—large.

Her depth of perception—limited.

Turning the corner, the horizontal star point bumped into a column of stuffed animals, spilling them all over the floor. While glancing at the spill, the opposite side knocked over another stand of ornaments. Heads turned at the sound of items crashing.

"Okay, alright—back it up starburst." Nan announced grabbing onto the closest point and steadying Marty on her feet.

She led Marty safely between the aisles, and around the counter to the carved wooden door leading outside to the townhouse's private courtyard.

"It was good to see you, Marty!" Nolan called out at the last second; heads turning again to watch her struggle in her wide costume through the narrow entryway.

"I'm just going to scratch his eyes—" Marty muttered trying to turn back. Nan gave a final *heave-ho* and pushed her through the doorway.

The courtyard had a small office shed with staff bathroom and stairwell which led to the three apartments above. Nan occupied the second-floor apartment, Chestnut the third, and Marty the attic at the very top. Marty would always be eternally grateful for Nan, who adopted her as a child and begrudgingly accepted help in the store in return for renting the top floor.

Chestnut appeared minutes later with a large smile, her eyes bright and fresh. "That Nolan sure is charming. He got the whole store to rally together and sort out the mess of ornaments. It's saved us hours!"

"Isn't he a God." Marty hissed sarcastically and threw down the warm compress Nan had pressed into her hands and pushed against her left eye—an unfortunate bystander in Marty's attempt at navigating out of the costume.

"I don't know what you have against him; the kids love him!" Chestnut continued. "During the *Handbell Choir Concert*, he showed up with gifts for everyone in attendance."

"He's annoying." Marty mumbled. She grabbed a bowl of mixed nuts off the desk and ate a handful while glaring at the closed door behind which she knew Nolan was schmoozing the crowd.

"He's jolly. Something you could aim to be." Nan waved away Marty's response before turning to Chestnut. "What are you doing out here? Who is watching the counter?"

"Nolan." Chestnut shrugged in response.

"I supposed that's okay." Nan nodded with a defeated sigh then headed up the stairs.

"What—Nan, you can't be serious, Nolan can't work the front counter!" Marty insisted. She followed Nan but stopped at the bottom of the stairs, pleading up at the woman with oversized eyes.

"I'm going to lie down; I'm getting too old. If *you* won't help Chezi, then Nolan can do it in between his shifts playing Sant—"

"Shhh—" both Chestnut and Marty responded before she could finish the name.

"Don't let her burn it down," Nan pointed at Marty while instructing Chestnut as she disappeared into her apartment.

"It would be easier if you'd help the Adventurers yourself." Chestnut sighed.

"Absolutely not," Marty shook her head and stuffed another handful of nuts into her mouth, annoyed at the thought of Nolan working with them. Her love for the old woman was the only reason she dressed up as ornaments every day: and *attempted* to partake in the village lifestyle. She still wouldn't help the Adventurers. She drew the line at *actually* being accommodating.

"You seem awfully flustered whenever he's around." Chestnut smirked, eyebrows raised.

"There's something—off—about him." Marty walked across the courtyard and creaked open the door to the Ornament shop. Peeking through to spy on Nolan; he stood behind the counter, laughing with a few female Adventurers that looked barely out of whelping school themselves.

The same age Nolan looked on his first day at Pole. He'd been there for weeks and was becoming quite burdensome, especially after learning when Marty worked. He stopped by daily during her lunch break to see if she wanted to do an activity—always a no—and again, at the end of her shift, to ask her to dinner.

At first, she assumed he only did this because Mayor Kringle had made the initial introductions—she understood how people viewed that as instant friendship—but she assured him, it wasn't. Cleo had generously thrown herself at him every opportunity she could; Santa's workshop had never received so many bakery items, delivered by hers truly.

But when Nolan continued to visit Marty and ask her *questions* about her interests and dislikes, she began to grow suspicious of his intentions. Marty hated overly nice people who weren't elves, especially the *extra* nice ones. It usually meant they were hiding something.

And if anyone knew about hiding, it was Marty.

Wednesday

It was extra cold for the *Winter Games* which were weathered whether the weather warranted it or not.

Marty wore her favorite costume; a puffy coat made of goose feathers in neon turquoise and pink, with a thick black boxy pattern. That morning she'd gone down the mountain slope just so she could get the appropriate amount of windburn on her face, outlining the thick goggles that now sat on top of her forehead, scrunching her hair back into tangles. The pants matched the coat and *swish-swish-swish*ed between her thighs when gliding across the store—which she did a lot because she liked to see the annoyance on the Adventurers' faces when she *swished* past. Sometimes she took her shoes off so she could slide easier along the wood floor in socks.

The *Winter Games* were a high attendance activity. Adventurers traveled far and wide from Other Worlds to take a chance at the slopes surrounding the little town. During the morning runs, professionals would compete for *Best Times*, *Best Performance*, and *Best Skills* in skiing or snowboarding followed by the amateur and beginners.

The afternoon found the skating rink expanded; the iron fences raised higher with plexi-glass coverings that separated the stadium risers. First, the *Kids Ice Capades* featured Junior and Intermediate Level figure skaters. Then came the Advanced and Professional Performances followed by the *Holiday Ice Spectacle:* a family-friendly performance showcasing the talent and hard work of the performers.

The day ended with an hour of *Free Skate* before the Zamboni cleaned the rink in preparation for the evening's highlight: *The Hockey Game.* It was held as the sun set in a sea of Red or White, depending on which team the Adventurers cheered for. They crowded the risers and bought paraphernalia of their favorite players.

Somehow, Nolan earned a spot on the Red Royal Elf team as captain. He sped around the rink, appearing weightless as if born in blades. His smile washed over the crowd in loud, roaring cheers of admiration. Circling, he raised his stick in the air amongst the cheers and chants of his name. At the end of the game, when he cinched the final goal—his team double-digits ahead of the other—they carried him off like a king, raising him high to celebrate. His hair gleamed with sweat when he removed his helmet to wave at the crowd, flipping it out of his eyes.

Marty fought a grin from her window seat. She sipped her tea and pulled the string on her blinds, rolling them all the way up so she had a clear view to watch the game. Rolling her eyes, as Nolan moved swiftly in and out of the other players. She was mesmerized by the sway of his hips as he circled the rink. The shine of his hair, forever lingering in his eyes when he flipped it, knowing it drove her crazy. The gleam of his white teeth when he looked up and smiled—just for her—knowing she watched. Every time he lifted his stick in the air and pointed it straight at her— silently dedicating each goal in her name, causing a roll of her eyes, a quickening of her heart, and a warm fluttering in her stomach.

The soft knock came later in the evening, and she answered. Irritated at the late hour but nervous, the pounding of her heart was a distraction, as she opened. He leaned against the doorframe, his broad shoulders filling the space, with muscled arms and a musky scent. She still didn't know what magic he used and for the moment, she didn't care.

Marty reached forward and took his hand, pulling him inside without a word. Words weren't needed when their stolen glances turned into urging looks, hesitant hands into roaming grabs, and whispered silences into lingering moans.

Words weren't needed with so many secrets between them.

Thursday

"It's counter-productive to claim you don't like someone then spend all day staring doe-eyed at them." Nan teased Marty who rolled her eyes, growling at the old woman.

Marty nibbled on her bottom lip; her hands clutched in front because the cylinder pieces of the Nutcracker costume prevented her from crossing her arms over her chest. She stood behind the counter, staring out the window at the *Santa Clause Games & Holiday Spirit Competition* taking place in the *Workshop* courtyard. From her position, she could clearly see Santa sitting on his throne, judging the *Look-A-Like Competition*, the *Fattest Santa Competition*, the *Cutest Baby Competition*, the *Best Beard Competition*, and finally the *Cheeriest Ho-Ho-Ho Competition*, every Thursday.

Nolan looked winded, and not from the cold air that blew through Main Square. He looked tired and out of breath, like he'd been running a marathon and paused long enough to catch it before continuing. Except he'd been sitting all morning.

He aged again, older, and not for the better. Handsome, but less put together, like he didn't care about making himself presentable. The need to impress and charm everyone around him faltered, which wasn't normal.

"I'm concerned." Marty muttered in response. A feather from the tin soldier hat flopped down in front of her eyes. She blew at it half-heartedly. "Help please."

Chestnut walked over and plucked the feather from her hat. She tucked it into Marty's jacket pocket with the others that had fallen then turned to stare out the window with her.

"He looks healthy, robust." Chestnut shrugged and turned away to help the line of customers.

Nan was behind the counter, wrapping boxes of presents for the Adventurers who waited, lingering about the store and picking up additional purchases. "No one is concerned but you, and only because he's the longest Santa we've ever had."

"You don't find that suspicious?" Marty glanced at the old woman and tsked. "Lift with your legs,"

"You come over here and lift this, so I don't have to anymore." Nan snapped in response, but Marty only raised a squeaky arm. "You look ridiculous, I can't believe you still wear that thing."

"I'm going to wear it every day now," Marty muttered and slowly shuffled robotically away from the window to bother Nan by the wrapping station.

"Will you just accept his proposal and go live a happy life." Nan huffed with a laugh and a shake of her head.

"Marriage would be easier if he told me his secret." Marty grabbed the end of a ribbon spool and slowly turned in a circle, the ribbon wrapping around her body.

"Everyone keeps secrets, even in a marriage between the best of friends—like your parents." Nan continued and pulled a pair of scissors tightly along the edge of the ribbon to curl the pieces.

"Those people are not friends." Marty barked a laugh at the ridiculous notion.

"*Your parents* have been alive several millennia; there are no two closer beings than the pair of them." Nan continued under her breath, her patience for Marty shorter than usual that day. Perhaps it was all the sulking Marty was doing. Chestnut claimed she was *pining* but she wasn't sure what that even felt like.

"How do you get someone to tell you secrets?" Marty was dizzy from spinning in a circle. The helmet slid down her eyes a few turns ago so she couldn't see how much ribbon she'd wrapped around herself by then.

"That would require talking, not just kissing!" Chezi interrupted.

"I've no idea what you mean." Marty scoffed dryly.

"Ach, stop that!" Nan finally realized the mess Marty created and howled in annoyance, grabbing the ribbon and halting Marty's steps with a lurching wobble. The helmet was ripped from her head and Nan's angry face, teasing eyes, filled Marty's vision. "You are a menace—and you need to grab onto that man—who miraculously finds you charming—and you must chain yourself to him for all eternity lest you continue to be my burden!"

"She means that with all the love in her heart!" Chestnut called from across the store.

Friday

Marty screamed when Nolan came into the shop. She hardly recognized his age and panicked by throwing six-inch wooden nutcrackers at him until he fled. Chestnut thought she was insane, and Nan scolded her for several minutes.

Nolan had grown into his part *too* comfortably. Marty didn't understand how no one else voiced concern about his changing appearance. His skin looked sickly, in the early stages of possible decomposition, pocked with spots. His once golden hair and beard were now white and thinning without its usual luster.

It confused and angered Marty. Something was happening that he wouldn't admit.

Nan worried about Marty. "Your mother wouldn't like this." She mumbled under her breath at how distraught Marty acted.

Marty didn't like it either. She'd never felt strongly about anyone in her life. She'd never wondered what they were thinking or how their day, as monotonous as they always were, turned out. But now she thought about such things and wondered them about Nolan.

And so, Marty did what her family did best in these situations.

She broke into a house.

Nolan was busy leading the *Midnight Stroll & Sing Caroling*. He and the villagers held lanterns while walking around the village seven times, singing songs for the Adventurers' enjoyment. Based on his decrepit appearance, she wasn't sure he would last the entire seven rounds.

Marty used this time to slip into the Mansion. She entered through the back door which she'd used a thousand times as a kid, grabbed a cookie from the kitchen before tiptoeing to the living room.

The furniture was the same, set up exactly like the Adventurers imagined. Two red chairs sat between an overstuffed couch; side tables covered in doilies with a perpetual plate of milk and cookies on top. A brick fireplace with roaring fire and iron faceplate lit a Christmas Tree in the corner with fake presents stacked beneath.

Marty dusted off the couch and sat down in the center cushion, her body sinking into the familiar deep seat. She tucked her legs underneath and folded her hands, making herself comfortable. A golden cuckoo-clock sat atop the mantle. She watched as the hand ticked down the seconds counting, three-two-one—

A mass of black ash dropped on top of the fire, extinguishing it immediately, followed by a pair of black boots. Their wearer landed with a great growl as he straightened and dusted himself off amongst curses.

"Fuck all." Nicholas gasped when he spotted Marty.

"Hey dad."

Nicholas

"Just like old times, huh?" Marty rolled her eyes and gave an overly sarcastic smile at her father, Nicholas Saint Claus.

Nicholas started his life as a lazy mortal who happened to be good at cards & charming goddesses, but ended life as an immortal—cursed to deliver hand-made toys—thanks to a rendezvous with Mistletoe's mother, who never quite got over the fact that he pretended not to remember her name the next morning.

"Nobody said we enjoyed old times," Nicholas barked in reply, his deep, baritone voice echoing through the house. It was built for him— the entire town of Pole—for Nicholas' humiliation and he spent the majority of the week away from the mansion, only required to return on Christmas Eve to deliver toys to the Adventurers while they slept.

"I need a favor."

"Straight to it, I see." Nicholas pretended to stab his heart and staggered into one of the red chairs where he collapsed dramatically.

"You don't stay long enough for a heart-to-heart." Marty sighed reminding her father about his important job that evening and that he avoided the town of Pole the other six days of the week.

"I stay as long as I'm wanted, nobody cares about Santa after they get their presents, you know that." He waved away her comment and grabbed a few cookies off the table. "How old are these? Doesn't matter, what can I help you with Mistletoe?"

"Will you wake up mom?"

Saturday

Marty looked out at the line of men, wrapped in thick blankets against the cold wind that swept down the mountains surrounding Pole. The winter storm blew across the rink over the huddled masses clenching lines, hoping to catch a tempting nibble from a fish below. Every Saturday the *Ice-Fishing Competition* took place in the center rink with men hunched over holes all day.

The men loved it while the women spent the time relaxing at the spa and the children terrorized the villagers with their new presents. By evening half of the Adventurers will leave— deciding it's easier to travel overnight when the sugar crash happens. The other half will leave in the morning after spending one last evening in town.

Marty pinched at the white bloomers itching underneath her checkered skirt. The sleeves of her blouse squeezed her armpits while the white lace around her collar choked her neckline. Marty leaned her weight against the shepherd's crook in her left hand to scratch her socks while wondering if she left the costume in a closet of fleas. She'd suffer the itch but couldn't bear to continue watching Nolan waste away.

Fetching the matching shawl for the shepherdess façade, she threw it over her shoulders and wrapped the ends around her head.

"You look like my grand babushka," Chestnut commented as Marty crouched, grabbing onto the lead of the three black and white sheep, Penny, Perry, and Dave, that she borrowed for the day.

"Your grand babushka is my favorite person." Marty replied which Chestnut knew was a joke because her grand babushka wasn't *anyone's* favorite person. "Please return the sheep to the stables."

"Mistletoe! You know I hate hooves!" Chezi whined but accepted the lead, shaking her head and waving Marty out the door to proceed with her terrorizing.

"Do you want to go on a sleigh ride?" Marty asked Nolan, leaning down to inspect the line in his hole.

"Oh, you're finally acquiescing to join this old geezer on a sleigh ride?" Nolan joked and looked up at her, his blue eyes still piercing her heart.

"Sure am, need help?" she offered her arm without waiting.

Nolan had really done a wonder on his joints as Santa. He should've stopped years ago but let the weeks fly by without accepting defeat. Finally, Mayor Kringle had to announce his forced retirement and a new Santa was hired.

Usually, the Santa's vacated Pole when they were replaced, but Nolan had been hanging around the village. It wasn't *technically* against the rules, since no one had ever done it. Most Santas were glad to leave after they served their agreed upon years. The music alone drove them crazy.

Marty walked the slow...slow...slow steps with Nolan to the waiting sleigh. A passing elf helped her load him into the seat, his body a lot thinner than she expected, and she tucked a blanket tightly around his lap for warmth.

"Careful of those hands, missy." Nolan joked with a wheezing laugh.

Marty rolled her eyes and tucked her arm through the crook of his elbow before nodding to the driver. The sleigh was pulled by two reindeer and driven by the Ghost of Christmas Spirit, a special favor to her family. Marty had chosen her mother's favorite place, a gazebo that stood in the middle of a circular clearing, surrounded by a ring of snow-covered spruce trees.

They were the last to arrive, just as Marty planned. Shadows moved about inside the gazebo, becoming more concrete as they drew close. Nolan sat up straighter, a bit of pep returning to his cheeks.

"Who's there?" he called, even though they weren't nearly close enough for anyone to hear.

"Recognize anyone?" Marty asked and saw that he was, indeed, getting a bit younger the closer they got to the gazebo.

"Ah, damn." Nolan sighed no longer squinting. Almost there; Marty made out the faces of her parents amongst the three waiting immortals. Nolan turned to Marty and grabbed her hands. "I suppose this isn't the best time to confess my deepest, darkest secret to you, is it?"

She met his eyes, the sharp blue of the ice he'd been fishing minutes earlier still there and rolled her own green. "It depends on if the secret has anything to do with escaping the fate of Father Time?"

"It might have something to do with that." Nolan nodded cheekily spurring another wheezing laugh. "It also has to do with not wanting to die. Life is beautiful—just like you."

He was growing young again, middle-aged and refined. His smile causing an eruption in her chest while opening a hole in her heart. Losing him might be the hardest thing she ever did.

"Quite the charmer, aren't you?" Marty responded unamused by his floundering.

"I had to try, one last time." He gave his classic, lop-sided flip of his hair.

The sleigh arrived and they exited together, hands clenched around each other's, fingers entwined, desperately clinging. Nolan led and stood in front of Marty, a bow toward each God.

"Who the hell are *you* to make me wait?" Father Time boomed down at his son.

The God wore a thick winter coat of silver, lined in white, decorated in embroidered stars with a belt pulled tightly around his waist. His pointed hood was nearly the same length as his silver beard with dark eyes glaring gloomily at his son. In his right hand he held a sharpened, silver scythe.

"Hello Mistletoe, my lovely girl." Gaia greeted holding her arm open for Marty to approach. Her mother looked ever gorgeous. Skin pale as snow lightly freckled, elegantly draped in a transparent green silk dress with golden locks trailing the ground hiding what bits the dress exposed. The Goddess held a staff carved from Hawthorn wood in her left hand and wrapped her right around Marty's back for a tight hug.

Marty hadn't seen her mother in a few years, the blink of an eye for an immortal. Not since her parents had their last *almost* torrid affair. They reunited every century or two and grew passionately in love before realizing they hated the other and would separate again.

"What's going on here?" Nolan asked looking between her mother, his father, and Nicholas. Marty stepped away from her mother and moved back to stand beside Nolan.

"Stop staring at my wife, Padre." Nicholas snapped toward the God. Father Times eyes shifted away from Gaia's body. Her mother wiped invisible crumbs from Nicholas' neatly trimmed beard. He was the only God dressed in a sharp, modern gray suit, his duties over for the year.

"Could someone please explain?" Nolan continued. Marty took his hand and squeezed their fingers together.

"Someone's late for their retirement party," Father Times hand waved his son up and down like a disappointed father.

"Not really keen on dying," Nolan retorted.

"Unfortunately for you, my son, you don't make those decisions, and seriously—" Time continued as if he wasn't talking about his son's *life*, "—you tried to hide from me *here* of all places?"

Father Time huffed and turned around in a circle, indicating the scenery.

"Where better to hide from Time then in a place where you don't exist?" Nolan shrugged as if the answer wasn't obvious. Marty thought it quite clever.

Pole resided in a time vortex, where it was always the Week Before Christmas. Every Sunday began on December 20th and every Saturday ended on December 26th. The days never differed, the schedule never changed and the weather was a constant snowstorm.

"You can't stop New Years Eve from happening by trying to dodge time." The old man continued with a strained laugh. The laugh became a gruff cough which turned into a wheeze. No one moved to help the immortal. "Your time is up—uh, Nick, Nate—"

"Nolan," he corrected, narrowing his eyes. Marty had to agree; Time was probably her most hated God.

Gaia rolled her eyes. "You've always been dramatic." Marty could tell from the tone of her mother's voice the Goddess grew agitated. Father Time probably shouldn't have insulted their surroundings.

"You'se called me here, remember?" Father Time pointed at her mother. Marty's eyebrows rose. Her mother could be...testy.

"Let's make a deal, Ralph." Gaia stepped forward, one arm lightly settled under her full breasts, the other bent upward as she contemplated the lesser God.

"You're foolish to make a bargain, especially for him." Time laughed and wiggled a thumb in Nolan's direction like a hitchhiker.

"I remember saying something very similar to Death about *you*," Gaia harrumphed. Time scowled at the Goddess and shifted his scythe between hands, uneasy at his choices.

"Immortals aren't supposed to make bargains for lesser Gods; they accept their fate— it's not good to upset the cosmos." A last attempt to plead his way out of the bargain.

"Oh, do stop it, Ralph," her mother interrupted again with a scoff. She threw her arms up in the air and turned to Nicholas who only shook his head at the Goddess' intervention. "You've plenty of other kids to sacrifice. Be a good lad and take a music mogul or politician, you've got a few hundred of those!"

"I told you not to fight it, Time," Nicholas directed his annoyance toward the God bearing the weight of his wife's wrath.

"They've fallen in love, and I'll not have you upsetting my daughter. Grant the boy immortality and punish him for his obsolesce," Gaia thumped Time across the head with her staff.

"This is cheating, I don't get nothing in return—" Time complained as Gaia thumped him again.

"You get to continue being fertile, avoiding your own expiration—lest you forget I could make you impotent. Then what year would be left but *you* one day?" Gaia threatened and gave several more thunks over his head for good measure.

Time grumbled once more but stalked over to the young couple. Marty shifted her stance in front of Nolan, not letting his father touch him with his scythe.

"Move girl, I'll not hurt him under your mother's watch." Time grumbled.

"I'll turn you into a newt." Her mother called in warning.

Marty held onto Nolan's arm and slowly moved around him, not letting go until she stood at his back—still attached to his hand.

"You'll have to release him lest you get hit yourself."

"She's already immortal, stop delaying and get on with it, Ralph!" Gaia commanded, her voice booming louder as her temper and impatience grew. Mother Nature was not always kind to Time.

The old man grumbled once more but stuck his arms out, hovering just above Nolan's shoulders. He spouted some ancient words, made several wide, circular hand movements, there was a flash of bright, white light and suddenly—

Sunday

Stepping outside smelled like snow. The cold winter breeze swept through Main Square as Mistletoe Saint Claus inhaled a deep breath; pine trees and cinnamon filling her senses. A snowflake landed against her eyelids; face pointed upward to feel the last warmth of the sun as it disappeared behind gray clouds.

Marty listened to the carolers singing as she walked along the ice rink. Mayor Kringle lit the Christmas Tree amongst a new crowd of Adventurers who *oohed* and *ahhed.* Carolers broke into song on cue, and the belltower gave five low tones—*gong, gong, gong, gong, gong*—signaling the evening hour.

She turned the corner and bumped into Cleo.

"Oh," Marty muttered clearing her throat and stumbling backwards.

"Ugh, Mistletoe—" Cleo began before Marty interrupted. "Sorry about that,"

"What?" Cleo stammered, her eyes wide in surprise.

"You look..." Cleo glanced Marty up and down with less of her usual sneer. "...nice, I supposed."

"Thank you," Marty turned away before felt compelled to continue speaking.

Marty picked up the sides of the blue ball gown and quickened her pace. Suddenly wishing she hadn't chosen a Princess costume. The gown, its volumes of silk, tulle and tight corset with sweetheart neckline, black ribbon tied around her neck, hair pinned up in a bun, felt like overkill.

She agreed to *one* sleigh ride.

Marty saw the back of Nolan's head and slowed her approach to appraise him. He was slightly taller, his back straight and broad, arm chiseled. His hair was light brown and clean-cut but long enough to run her fingers through.

And then he turned to face her—his eyes the same sharp blue as the frozen river. His smile, crooked beneath a peppered beard trimmed neatly around his lips. He looked refined and sexy. His features were smooth and sophisticated, his skin glowing amaretto with new immortality.

He smiled and lifted her into his arms, holding her waist tightly while spinning her in the air, haloed by the lights.

"Stop, you're doing a *thing*—put me down." Marty shrieked regrettably realizing how romantic the moment appeared.

"No, I get my moment." He insisted, hoisting her higher and holding her tighter.

Marty laughed and leaned closer, kissing the top of his head and running her hands through the strands, flipping the pieces that fell in his eyes off his forehead.

"Will it do?" he teased stopping and cradling her cheek, his voice deep and silky. Her stomach grew warm, and she squirmed, heart hammering against her chest when their eyes locked.

She wondered if *this* was what he felt when he looked at her. Instead of answering, she leaned forward, pressing her lips against his own.

"It'll do."

Acknowledgements

As always, thank you to my amazing son, without
whom my life would be boring.

Thank you to my little sister for always encouraging my
creativity and writing.

To Peaches for being the best friend and first reader I
could ever want as a writer. Thank you for
enthusiastically reading everything!

And finally, to all the December birthdays who hate the
Holiday because it overshadows us every year,
thanks for understanding!

Gigi Shoe earned a BS in English Education then achieved her MA in English Literature. Since 2011 she's taught middle school English and loves being the Mrs. Frizzle of Writing. She lives in the Midwest with a rowdy cast of family, friends, and four-legged creatures who can find her reading in the garden and daydreaming of other worlds.

www.ingramcontent.com/pod-product-compliance
Lightning Source LLC
Chambersburg PA
CBHW010745310726
48971CB00010B/2951